A Note from Michelle about
Calling All Planets

Hi! I'm Michelle Tanner. I'm nine years old. And I just did something really dumb. I promised my friends Evan and Lucas I would help them make a model of the solar system for the science contest. Then I promised my two best friends, Cassie and Mandy, exactly the same thing.

It gets worse! Because if anyone finds out I'm helping *two* teams win the same prize, I'll be in big trouble.

I can't even tell my family. And it's almost impossible to keep a secret from all of them!

There's my dad and my two older sisters, D.J. and Stephanie. But that's not all.

My mom died when I was little. So my uncle Jesse moved in to help Dad take care of us. So did Joey Gladstone. He's my dad's friend from college. It's almost like having three dads. But that's still not all!

First Uncle Jesse got married to Becky Donaldson. Then they had twin boys, Nicky and Alex. The twins are four years old now. And they're so cute.

That's nine people. Our dog, Comet, makes ten. Sure it gets kind of crazy sometimes. But I wouldn't change it for anything. It's so much fun living in a full house!

FULL HOUSE™
Michelle

Calling All Planets

Sarah Verney

A Parachute Press Book

Published by POCKET BOOKS
New York   London   Toronto   Sydney   Tokyo   Singapore

This book is a work of fiction. Names, characters, places and incidents
are products of the author's imagination or are used fictitiously. Any
resemblance to actual events or locales or persons, living or dead, is
entirely coincidental.

A MINSTREL PAPERBACK *Original*

A Minstrel Book published by
POCKET BOOKS, a division of Simon & Schuster Inc.
1230 Avenue of the Americas, New York, NY 10020

A PARACHUTE PRESS BOOK

READING Copyright © and ™ 1997 by Warner Bros.

FULL HOUSE, characters, names and all related indicia are
trademarks of Warner Bros. © 1997.

ISBN: 0-671-00365-8

First Minstrel Books printing March 1997

10 9 8 7 6 5 4 3 2 1

A MINSTREL BOOK and colophon are registered trademarks of
Simon & Schuster Inc.

Cover photo by Schultz Photography

Printed in the U.S.A.

Calling All Planets

Chapter

1

♥ *Slurp!*

Comet licked Michelle Tanner across the face.

She sat up in bed and stared down at the golden retriever. He thumped his tail against the floor.

"Hey, Comet," nine-year-old Michelle whispered. She leaned down and scratched him between the ears. "You know you aren't supposed to be in here."

Comet gave a little whine. He picked up his favorite green tennis ball and handed it

1

to Michelle. "And we both know we aren't supposed to play with this in the house."

Michelle tossed the ball out the open door of the bedroom she shared with her thirteen-year-old sister, Stephanie. Comet bounded after it.

"Michelle! Telephone," her father called from downstairs. "When you're through, come down for breakfast. My raspberry pop-up pancakes are almost ready!"

Every Sunday morning, Danny Tanner tried out a new recipe. Good thing Dad loves to cook, Michelle thought. Because there are a *lot* of people to feed in *this* house.

"Okay," Michelle shouted. She ran to the phone on the hall table and picked it up. "Hello?"

"Hi, it's Lucas." Lucas Hamilton sat three desks away from Michelle in their fourth-grade class.

"What's up?" Michelle asked. She was really curious. Lucas had never called her on the phone before.

"I wanted to know if you would paint something for me," Lucas began.

Comet dropped the tennis ball at Michelle's feet and whined. He nudged her with his cold nose. He whined again. She picked up the ball and rolled it down the stairs so she could talk.

"Hey!" Stephanie called from downstairs. "Watch out up there! You almost hit me!"

"Oops! I didn't mean to!" Michelle yelled back. She brushed her strawberry-blond hair out of her face.

"Didn't mean to what?" Michelle's eighteen-year-old sister, D.J., asked. She came out of the bathroom with a towel wrapped around her wet brown hair.

"One second, Lucas," Michelle said into the phone.

"I didn't mean to hit Stephanie," Michelle explained.

Alex and Nicky, Michelle's four-year-old twin cousins, ran down the hall. "You hit Stephanie? Why?" Alex asked.

"Did you hurt her?" Nicky said. His lower lip started to tremble. He always cried if someone else got hurt.

Michelle sighed. I'd better explain before he starts to cry, she thought. She leaned down to Nicky. "I didn't hurt anyone, Nicky. I rolled Comet's ball down the stairs and it almost hit Stephanie."

"Michelle, please don't throw the ball in the house!" Danny called from downstairs.

"Michelle, are you there?" Lucas asked.

Michelle jumped. She almost forgot about Lucas! "I'm here," Michelle answered.

"It sounds like you're having a party," he said.

"No, it's not a party. It's always like this around here," Michelle told him.

The Tanner household was pretty noisy.

Especially when everyone was home—like now.

Besides Stephanie, D.J., and the twins, there was her dad's best friend, Joey Gladstone. He moved in to help Danny after Michelle's mom died. That made seven people, including Michelle. The twins' parents, Michelle's uncle Jesse and aunt Becky, made nine.

Comet ran back upstairs with the tennis ball. If you counted dogs, and Michelle did, that made ten family members. It was a *very* full house.

"I wanted to know if you would paint something for me and Evan," Lucas began again. Lucas and Evan Burger were best friends. Evan was in Michelle's class too.

"Sure," Michelle answered. She loved art. "What do you want me to paint?"

"Something for our science project," Lucas told her.

"Science project? We don't have a project due," Michelle said. "Do we?"

"Not for class, for the science contest," Lucas explained.

"What science contest?" Michelle felt even more confused.

"This company called Microsolid is holding it. It's going to be great. If we win, we get to go to Sacramento and compete with kids from all over California. And with you on our team—"

"Michelle, breakfast," Danny called.

"I have to go," Michelle told Lucas. "Maybe you should find someone else. I'm not that great at science."

"But you're the best artist in the whole class!" Lucas protested. "Evan and I will do the science. You do the artwork."

Michelle bounced from foot to foot. Her dad would go nuts if she let her breakfast get cold. But she couldn't decide if she wanted to be on Lucas's team.

"Come on. Promise you'll do it. It will be fun!" Lucas insisted.

"Okay, I promise," Michelle said. Lucas and Evan were cool. It probably would be fun to work with them. Even if it did involve science.

"Great! See you tomorrow!" Lucas hung up, and Michelle ran downstairs to try her dad's pancakes.

"Michelle! The bell is about to ring. Why are you so late?" Michelle's best friend, Mandy Metz, asked on Monday morning.

"We didn't want to go in without you," Michelle's other best friend, Cassie Wilkins, added. They stood in the hall outside Mrs. Yoshida's fourth-grade classroom.

What great friends, Michelle thought. "I'm late because I had to chase Comet around the house. He took my scrunchie," she told Mandy and Cassie. "My favorite

7

one—the one with the pink polka dots! He got it all drooly too!"

"Dogs drool and cats rule," Cassie joked. She had two Persian cats and thought they were the best pets in the world.

The bell rang, and Michelle and her friends hurried inside. Lucas gave her a high-five as she walked by his desk, and she remembered their phone call on Sunday. I can't believe I'm on a science team, she thought as she sat down.

"Before we begin this morning, I want to make an announcement," Mrs. Yoshida said after she called roll. "Microsolid, one of the biggest science and technologies companies, is holding a science contest for kids between eight and twelve years old. They want to encourage students to learn about science—and maybe even work as scientists when they grow up."

Boy, this science contest sounds serious, Michelle thought. She felt a little nervous.

8

Don't worry, she told herself. Lucas and Evan are handling the science stuff.

"There is still time to sign up and prepare a project," Mrs. Yoshida continued. "And I'll be happy to help anyone who decides to enter."

Evan grinned at Michelle from across the room. "We're going to win!" he mouthed.

"Will you be my partner, Mrs. Y.?" Jeff Farrington called out. Jeff never stopped joking.

"I *am* short," she answered. "But I don't think anyone will believe I'm under twelve!"

Michelle laughed. Mrs. Yoshida could be as funny as Jeff sometimes.

"Now get out your history books and turn to page forty-seven," her teacher instructed.

A folded square of light blue paper landed on Michelle's desk as Mrs. Yoshida began to talk about the Oregon Trail. Michelle swept the note into her lap and unfolded it slowly.

On the paper was a little drawing of three

girls standing around a bubbling test tube. Each girl had a big first place ribbon in her hand. "You, me, and Cassie at the contest," read the note underneath.

Michelle gulped. Her friends wanted to enter the science contest too?

Oh, no! Michelle thought. I'm already on a team. How can I be on two teams at once?

Chapter

2

♥ "So, what are we going to do for the science contest?" Cassie asked at lunchtime.

Michelle bit into the cucumber, cheese, and tomato pita sandwich her dad had packed. She didn't want to answer Cassie. How could she tell her best friends she couldn't join their team?

"We have to come up with something really neat to win," Mandy said. She took a bite of the pizza the cafeteria served that day.

"Michelle? What do you think?" Cassie asked.

Michelle took a big bite of her sandwich. She held up one finger to show that she couldn't answer until she finished chewing. She didn't know what else to do.

This is stupid, she thought. I can't keep my mouth stuffed full of food for the next two weeks. I have to tell them the truth. She swallowed and took a deep breath.

"I can't be on your team," Michelle blurted out.

"What? Why not?" Cassie asked.

"Because I'm already on another team," Michelle answered miserably.

"What?" Cassie and Mandy cried at the same time.

"Lucas asked me yesterday and I promised to be on his team."

"But *we're* your best friends," Mandy protested.

"I didn't know you wanted to enter the science contest," Michelle explained.

"I didn't know about it until today," Cassie said.

"Me either. It won't be as much fun if we can't work on a project together," Mandy said.

"Come on, Michelle, best friends stick together," Cassie added. "Tell Lucas you have to switch."

"But I promised," Michelle said.

"Well, just un-promise him," Cassie told her.

Michelle frowned. Her uncle Jesse always said breaking a promise was wrong. "I can't un-promise," she insisted. "There's no such thing as an un-promise!"

What am I going to do? Michelle thought. I can't quit Lucas and Evan's team, but I really want to join Cassie and Mandy's team.

That gave her a great idea.

"I've got it! I'll be on both teams! There are no rules against that, are there?" Michelle exclaimed.

She reached for her sandwich. She felt great now that she had the perfect solution. This way, nobody would be angry at her. I'm a genius, Michelle thought.

Michelle took a regular-sized bite of her sandwich. Then she noticed that her friends weren't eating their pizza. Cassie and Mandy looked unhappy.

"The science contest is only two weeks away," Mandy said. "You won't have time to work on both projects."

"Besides, it wouldn't be fair for you to help another team win," Cassie added.

"Let Lucas find someone else," Mandy said.

"Think how much fun it will be when we win and get to go all the way to Sacramento together!" Cassie chimed in.

Michelle sighed. She never thought it would feel so awful to be wanted by so many people.

"Look, Lucas is waving at you," Cassie told her.

Michelle turned around and saw Lucas and Evan three tables away. She waved back.

"Tell him now, so he can find someone else," Mandy urged.

Michelle took a deep breath. She stood up and walked slowly to Lucas's table. Mandy is right, Michelle told herself. If I tell Lucas now, he'll have lots of time to find someone else.

But she didn't want to tell him. She wanted to turn around and run back to Cassie and Mandy's table.

Too late.

"Listen to this. We want to do a volcano," Evan exclaimed before Michelle could say a word. He slid down to make room for her on the bench.

Michelle sat down. "I can't be on—"

"We'll make it erupt with lava," Lucas interrupted.

"I can't—" Michelle tried again. She noticed Cassie and Mandy staring at her from their table. Her stomach flip-flopped.

"Yeah! We'll make some really oozy stuff that shoots out all over the place." Evan wiggled his fingers in front of Michelle's face.

"It will be so cool!" Lucas cried. "Don't you think a volcano is a great idea, Michelle?"

Michelle remembered how many volcanoes she had seen at last year's school science fair. Lucas and Evan would never win with something everyone else always did.

"That's boring," she said before she could stop herself. "Every year someone makes a volcano."

"Well, what do you think we should do?" Lucas frowned.

"I don't know. What about something with atoms or molecules . . ."

Wait, Michelle thought. This *isn't* what I'm supposed to be talking to them about. She glanced over at Cassie and Mandy. Mandy gave her a "go ahead and tell him" look.

"I can't be on your team," Michelle blurted out.

"What?" Lucas cried.

"I'm sorry. I'm really sorry. But Cassie and Mandy want me to be on their team and they're my best friends and—"

"No way!" Lucas said. "I asked you first. You promised!"

"Can't you find someone else? Please? I'll help you find someone else," Michelle offered.

"But no one is as good at art as you!" Evan said.

"And you owe me a favor. Remember? I gave you two of my best bugs for our insect lesson," Lucas said.

"I remember," Michelle answered.

"So you have to be on our team," Lucas insisted. "Okay?"

Michelle stared down at the cafeteria table. "Okay, okay," she whispered.

"Great!" Lucas said.

"Can we start working tomorrow?" Evan asked.

"I guess," Michelle said glumly.

"Can we work at your house—since you'll need your art stuff?" Lucas asked.

"I guess," Michelle answered. "See you later," she mumbled.

This is the worst day of my whole life, Michelle thought as she stood up and shuffled back to her table. Cassie and Mandy both had big smiles on their faces. They think I quit Lucas's team, she realized.

"Well?" Cassie asked as soon as Michelle sat down at their table. "Did you tell him?"

"I talked to him," she said. That was the truth, she told herself. Just not the *whole* truth.

"Was he mad?" Cassie asked.

"No," Michelle said.

"Good," Mandy said. "Then everything is perfect!"

How did I get myself into this mess? Michelle thought. And how am I ever going to get out of it?

Chapter

3

♥ "Aren't you glad you switched teams?" Cassie asked.

"Uh, yeah," Michelle replied. It wasn't exactly true that she switched teams. But it wasn't really a lie either.

All Evan and Lucas want is some artwork, she told herself. I'll do a few posters for them, and spend the rest of my time working with Cassie and Mandy. That seems fair. It's not like I'm really on the boys' team.

"Great!" Mandy high-fived Cassie. "We

couldn't have had a team without you!" Mandy exclaimed. "You're our best friend."

"So what should our project be?" Cassie asked.

"I've got an idea," Mandy said. "Let's do the solar system! We could make a model— and Michelle could paint all of the planets."

"Wow! That's great!" Michelle exclaimed. When she was little, her uncle Jesse used to read to her from a picture book about the planets. Then Joey would make up all these goofy alien characters.

Michelle could still remember how beautiful the drawings of the planets were. Making a model solar system would be so much fun. "We'll definitely win with this project!" she said. She couldn't wait to start working on it.

Cassie held up her milk carton. "To our project!" she cried.

Michelle and Mandy bumped their cartons against Cassie's. "To our project!" they repeated.

Michelle knew she would have to tell Cassie and Mandy about doing posters for the boys. And she would—later.

"I still think a volcano is the best idea," Evan said as he doodled on a piece of paper. He sat at the Tanners' kitchen table with Michelle and Lucas.

"The best idea for what?" Joey asked as he wandered into the kitchen.

"We're picking a project for the Microsolid science contest," Michelle explained.

"I want to make a volcano!" Evan told him.

"Ah—a volcano," Joey said. He started making a sandwich. "The judges will *erupt* into applause!"

Michelle giggled. Joey was a stand-up comic. He never stopped kidding around and talking in funny voices.

"I don't want to do a volcano. Why don't we make some kind of a laser?" Lucas suggested.

"How do you make a laser?" Evan asked.

Lucas shrugged. "I don't know," he said.

Michelle sighed. She wished Evan and Lucas would make up their minds. She wanted to do her posters for them quickly. Then she could spend all her time working on the solar system with Mandy and Cassie.

"Maybe we could do something about the dinosaurs," Evan said.

Comet padded into the kitchen. He stared at the slice of bread in Joey's hand.

"Mine," Joey told him. He wrapped his arms around the bread and held it close to his chest.

"Oh, he can have a little piece," Michelle said. "Right, Comet?"

"Comet!" Lucas cried. "That's it!"

"That's *what?*" Evan asked.

"Our project," Lucas explained. "We can do a solar system. With planets and the sun and comets and stuff!"

"That's a great idea," Evan agreed.

"No!" Michelle yelled. "I mean, not such a great idea."

Evan and Lucas both stared at her. Michelle could feel her cheeks growing red.

"What's wrong with it?" Lucas asked.

"Well, everybody does solar systems," Michelle told them.

"Everybody who?" Lucas asked.

"You know—everybody everybody," Michelle said. "Why don't we do a . . . um, a weather project!"

"A weather project?" Evan repeated. "Nah. I like the solar system better."

"So do I," Joey put in. He tossed Comet a piece of bread.

Thanks, Joey, Michelle thought.

"Hi, everyone! What's up?" D.J. asked as she strolled into the kitchen.

"Hi, Deej," Michelle said. "We're trying to pick a topic for our science project. Don't you think a weather project would be cool?"

D.J. wrinkled her nose. "It sounds kind of complicated," she answered.

Thanks, D.J., Michelle thought.

"What do you think of the solar system?" Lucas asked.

"That's a great idea," D.J. said.

Lucas turned to Michelle. "See? I told you!"

"So, we'll do the solar system!" Evan cried.

Michelle slid down in her chair. "Thanks a lot, Comet," she muttered. "You gave them the idea."

Now what was she supposed to do? Maybe I should just tell them the truth, she thought.

"Um . . . I think Cassie and Mandy are doing the solar system," Michelle admitted.

She held her breath and waited to see what Lucas would say. He would never want to use someone else's idea, would he?

"That doesn't matter," Lucas said. "Ours will be better. We can definitely beat Cassie and Mandy!"

Chapter
4

♥ "Here—blow this up." Lucas handed Michelle a green balloon.

Michelle shook her head. "I'm working on this map-of-the-solar-system poster. I'm the art person, remember?"

Danny Tanner slid a cake pan into the oven. "Give some to me," he volunteered. "I'll blow up a few for you."

"Thanks," Lucas answered.

POP! The balloon Evan was blowing up burst.

"Are you positive balloons are a good

idea?" Michelle asked. She and Lucas and Evan sat around the Tanner kitchen table the next day after school, working on their project.

"Sure," Lucas said. He took a deep breath and blew up the purple balloon in his hand.

Michelle held out a bag of Styrofoam balls. "I bought these yesterday. I thought you guys could use them for planets."

She would do anything to move the guys along faster. The sooner they got this project finished, the more time she could spend on her *real* project—the Cassie-Mandy-Michelle solar system!

Why can't they see making planets out of balloons won't work? Michelle thought grumpily. So far every single planet had popped!

Evan caught a blue balloon before it rolled off the table. "Maybe she's right about using those little balls," he told Lucas.

"I agree!" Danny said. "I can't blow up

one more balloon or *I'll* pop! You kids call me if you need any more help. Anything but balloon-blowing!" he added.

"Okay, Dad," Michelle answered. "Thanks." She watched her father head into the living room.

POP!

Michelle jumped as another balloon broke. "Comet!" she cried. Comet held a popped balloon in his mouth, and he looked frightened. He ran to hide in a corner of the kitchen.

Michelle hurried over to him. "Poor puppy, that scared you, didn't it?"

"Can't you keep him out of here?" Evan asked. "He'll pop all of them!"

POP! Another balloon broke.

"Comet didn't do that," Michelle pointed out.

"I did," Lucas admitted. He held up a broken balloon and the piece of wire he had been trying to wrap around the top.

"Maybe we *should* use the Styrofoam balls," he went on. "I just thought the balloons would look better since they are different sizes and colors."

The phone rang. Michelle patted Comet one more time. Then she walked across the kitchen to answer it.

"Hello?" she said. She watched as Lucas and Evan ripped open the bag of Styrofoam balls.

"Hi, Michelle," said a cheerful voice on the phone. Cassie!

"Um, hi, Cassie," Michelle answered.

Lucas glanced up from the wire he was bending. Michelle turned her back to him and spoke softly into the phone. "What's up?" she asked her best friend.

"Can Mandy and I come over after dinner?" Cassie asked. "We need to start working on our solar system. We really have to start now if we're going to have a great project ready in time."

29

"Uh . . . okay. That sounds good. But I've got to go right now," Michelle said into the phone. "See you later."

Michelle hung up and sat back down at the table. Lucas and Evan had chosen one Styrofoam ball for the sun. Now they were connecting smaller balls to it with wires.

"There's something wrong with it," Lucas said.

"Yeah, it doesn't look like the planets are going around the sun. They're just kind of sticking out of it," Evan agreed.

"What do you think, Michelle?" Lucas asked.

Michelle wanted to tell him it looked great, wonderful, terrific. Anything that would get him and Evan out of her house. "It looks really . . . um . . ."

She couldn't do it. She couldn't tell them their model looked good this way. "Pretty bad," she admitted.

"Yeah," Evan said.

"I've got it!" Lucas shouted suddenly. "We'll make a mobile. We'll hang the planets from pieces of wood with fishing line."

"That's a great idea!" Evan said.

"We can hang the mobile over our display table," Lucas said. "Then we can use the top of the table for the rest of our project."

"Too bad the mobile will just be hanging there," Evan complained. "It would be so cool if we could get it to spin."

Michelle frowned. "I've got it! We can use an electric tie rack!" she cried.

"What's that?" Evan asked.

"My dad has one," Michelle said. "It's this thing you hang your ties from that spins around when you flip a switch."

"Perfect!" Lucas cried. "We can hang the sun from the middle, and the planets from each of the little tie hangers. The planets will look like they're rotating by themselves. You're a genius, Michelle!"

31

It felt good coming up with that idea, Michelle thought. Like getting an A on a test.

"And we thought you'd be good only at the art part of the project!" Evan added.

Oh, no! Michelle thought. What did I just do?

I just broke a promise to my two best friends, she answered herself. Her stomach turned over. I just gave our competition a super-great idea! That's a million times worse than doing some posters for them.

And she hadn't even told Cassie and Mandy about the posters yet!

"I've got to get home," Lucas said. He grabbed the half-empty bag of balloons and stuffed them in his backpack. "I still wish we could have different-colored planets."

"We can," Evan announced. He grinned at Michelle.

No, Michelle thought. Oh, no. Don't say it.

"Michelle can paint the Styrofoam balls!"

Chapter 5

❤ *Ding-dong!*

Michelle jumped when the doorbell rang. It must be Cassie and Mandy! Michelle thought. They're early! She glanced at the clock on her dresser. No, they're right on time, she realized. I've been working longer than I thought.

After Evan and Lucas left, she started work painting the first planet. She managed to do a little more after dinner.

Michelle studied the Styrofoam ball she'd painted with pastel blue and white swirls.

The model Earth. It turned out good, Michelle decided.

She stuck the model planet under her bed. She couldn't let Cassie and Mandy see it. They would think she made it for them!

"Michelle! Cassie and Mandy are here," D.J. called from downstairs. "They're coming up!"

Michelle arranged her paints neatly. She didn't want it to look as if she'd just finished using them.

"Hi, Michelle," Cassie said. She came in the door carrying a plastic bag bulging with Styrofoam balls.

Michelle's throat went dry. "Hi," Michelle greeted her friends. "What are those for?"

"We're going to use these balls to make a model of the solar system," Mandy explained. "Cassie came up with the idea."

Oh, no! Michelle thought. They're planning to make a model just like Lucas and Evan's. I have to talk them out of it!

"Maybe we shouldn't make a model," Michelle suggested. "There will be tons of models entered in the contest, I bet. Maybe we can just do a . . . a chart of the planets or something."

"No, we need a model!" Cassie exclaimed. "But a chart is a great idea. It will make our project even better. You can work on it while we put together the model."

Michelle sighed. She couldn't tell her friends about Lucas and Evan's model without admitting that she had helped the other team. I've got to find a way out of this mess, she thought as she pulled a piece of poster board out of her closet.

But there is no way out, she realized. The only thing I can do is tell Cassie and Mandy the truth. No matter how horrible it is.

I'll tell them in a minute, Michelle decided. I'll just work on the chart a little first.

When Michelle was about halfway finished, she swallowed hard. She opened her mouth to speak—and a Styrofoam ball bounced across the floor. It hit the corner of the poster board and smeared the paint.

"Hey!" Michelle exclaimed. "Be careful!"

"I'm sorry," Cassie answered. "But this is driving me nuts!"

Michelle gazed over at her friends. They both frowned as they stared at their model—a bunch of Styrofoam balls stuck together in a straight line. The ball that was supposed to be the sun was glued to a wooden base.

"The planets don't line up like that," Michelle pointed out. "They all revolve around the sun at different speeds."

"I know that," Cassie answered.

"You need to make the planets look like they're going around the sun," Michelle went on.

"That's what we've been *trying* to do," Mandy complained.

This is bad, Michelle thought. It would be time for Cassie and Mandy to go home soon.

And her *real* team's project looked worse than her *fake* team's project!

"We have to use something instead of the wood block," Michelle announced.

"Like what?" Cassie asked.

"Well, something that you could spin around," Michelle explained. "To make it look like the planets are moving around the sun."

"Like what?" Cassie repeated.

This is the worst, Michelle thought. She didn't want to give away Lucas's idea. That wouldn't be fair.

But she had to help Cassie and Mandy. They were her teammates!

"What spins around?" Michelle asked.

"Tops spin," Mandy answered.

"Pinwheels spin," Cassie said.

This is going to take forever, Michelle thought.

"Hey, I know!" Cassie exclaimed. "Spice racks."

"That's great!" Michelle cried. "That could work like the tie rack!"

"What tie rack?" Mandy asked.

Oh, no! Michelle thought. I didn't mean to say that. "Um, my dad's tie rack sort of spins," she explained. "But it's not as good as a spice rack."

"A tie rack . . . wait a minute." Michelle could see Cassie thinking. "A tie rack is electric, right?" she asked. "My dad has one too."

"That's perfect!" Mandy said. "If it's electric, we can turn it on and it will spin by itself. If we use the spice rack, we have to push it to make it spin."

"Michelle, you're a genius!" Cassie cried. "So we'll hang your planets from the mini hangers and the tie rack will spin them around. That's a great idea!"

"Cassie, your mother is here to pick you and Mandy up," Danny called from downstairs.

Time for them to go already. And Michelle hadn't said anything about Lucas and Evan. It felt so bad spending time with her best friends—and keeping such a big secret from them.

But what could I do? Michelle asked herself. If I was only painting posters, I could tell them. But I already helped Lucas and Evan figure out how to make their model— even though I didn't mean to. And now I'm painting planets for them!

" *'Bye,* Michelle," Cassie said. Mandy giggled.

"What's so funny?" Michelle asked.

"That's the third time I said it," Cassie replied.

"Michelle hasn't come back from outer space," Mandy teased.

Michelle forced herself to smile at her friends. "See you tomorrow," she called as they made their way out the front door.

39

She shut the door and threw herself down on the living room couch.

She felt so glad the day was almost over. Comet trotted up to her and rested his chin on her knee. "If everyone finds out what I'm doing, they'll all hate me!" she told him. "But no matter what happens, you'll still love me. Right, boy?" she asked.

Comet dropped his ball into her lap. "Comet, you know we can't play ball in the—oh, no!" Michelle cried. "That's not a ball. That's my model Earth!"

Chapter 6

♥ "Comet destroyed the Earth on Wednesday," Michelle told Evan and Lucas. "I'm not letting him in the kitchen while we're working today."

The three of them headed straight to the Tanners' after school on Monday. Michelle hoped they would be able to finish their project that afternoon. That way she could spend the rest of the week working for Cassie and Mandy.

"What are we going to do without the Earth?" Evan cried.

"Don't worry," she said. "I made an even better one. I'll show you later." Michelle thought of the box of painted planets in her room upstairs. They were really beautiful— she had spent all weekend painting them for the Lucas-Evan solar system.

Lucas and Evan sat down at the kitchen table and spread out their supplies. "This is going to be the coolest solar system at the fair!" Lucas said. "Look at this article I found about Neptune."

Ding-dong!

"Michelle! Will you get the door?" Joey called from downstairs.

As soon as she opened the kitchen door, Comet tried to squeeze through it. "Comet! Stay out!" Michelle cried. "You can't have any more of my science project!" She held him by the collar as she pulled the kitchen door shut behind her.

Ding-dong!

"I'm coming!" Michelle yelled. She ran to the front door and pulled it open.

"Hi, Michelle," Cassie said.

Oh, no! What was Cassie doing here?

"Hi," Mandy said, appearing behind Cassie.

Michelle's heart pounded as her friends pushed their way into the house. I really messed up this time! she thought. How could I forget Cassie and Mandy were coming over?

"Um . . . let's go upstairs," Michelle said quickly. She couldn't let her friends find out that Lucas and Evan were working in the kitchen!

"I'm really hungry, Michelle," Mandy said. "Can I get a piece of fruit first?" She started for the kitchen. Michelle jumped in front of her.

"No!" she cried. "I mean, I . . . I just mopped the floor. We can't go in there until it dries."

Mandy and Cassie stared at her in surprise. "Why were you mopping?" Cassie asked.

"Um, because I spilled some . . . mustard on the floor. And Dad hates it when the floor is dirty." Michelle couldn't believe she was lying to her best friends like this. This was awful!

"I know. You go on upstairs, and I'll bring some snacks up to you," Michelle suggested. If she didn't get back into the kitchen quick, one of the boys might come looking for her.

Cassie and Mandy appeared even more surprised. Uh-oh, what did I say wrong? Michelle wondered.

"But how can you go in there if the floor is wet?" Mandy asked.

"Um, my footprints are already on the floor," Michelle said. "So it's okay if I walk on it."

Her friends glanced at each other. They think I'm crazy, Michelle thought. Her heart pounded double time in her chest. They know I'm lying!

"Okay," Cassie said. "I guess you know what you're doing," She started up the stairs with Mandy behind her.

That was close! Michelle thought. Now I just have to keep Cassie and Mandy away from Lucas and Evan, and everything will be fine—I hope!

"Michelle?" Cassie called just as Michelle put her hand on the kitchen door.

Michelle jumped away from the door. "What?" she cried. Could Evan and Lucas hear her?

Cassie gave her a puzzled look. "Can you bring some aluminum foil when you come up?" she asked.

"Oh," Michelle said. "Yeah. Sure."

Cassie frowned at her for a second, then shrugged and continued upstairs. Michelle sighed and pushed open the kitchen door. "Stay out, Comet," she ordered. She had enough problems without the dog getting in the way.

"What are you doing?" Michelle asked. Evan and Lucas sat hunched over their solar system, untying the planets from the tie rack.

"We wanted to see how it looks with colored string instead of fishing wire."

"That's a great idea, Lucas," Michelle said. "But won't it take longer to finish if you take it all apart? We would have to build the whole thing again today."

"What's the rush?" Lucas asked. "We have all week."

Michelle groaned. "But I have so much work to do this week," she complained.

"What do you have to do?" Evan asked.

"Just homework and stuff. And Dad wants me to clean out my closet. Plus I promised the twins I would play zoo with them, and I have to give Comet a bath," she lied.

"We can try to hurry," Evan said. "Where are the planets you made?"

The planets? Oh, no! Michelle thought. The planets were upstairs with Cassie and Mandy.

"I'll go get them," she told the boys. "The pastel paints I used worked great."

She sped back up the stairs. Michelle stepped into her room. Cassie and Mandy turned to her. I'll have to sneak the planets out of my room very carefully, Michelle thought. It will be tricky, but I think I can do it.

"Michelle, these are incredible!" Cassie cried, holding the box filled with Lucas and Evan's painted planets. "We're definitely going to win now!"

Chapter

7

♥ Michelle stared at the planets she had painted for the other team. How many other things are going to go wrong before this contest is over? she thought.

"It really is amazing!" Mandy exclaimed. "How did you paint the little rings on this one? They're great!"

"I can't believe you did all this work on one planet," Cassie added. "It must have taken forever."

"Did you see this one?" Mandy asked. She held up the Earth that Michelle had painted after Comet ate the first one. "I thought you were going to paint the planets solid colors," Mandy said.

"I was," Michelle murmured. I have to tell them the truth, she thought. Tell them those aren't their planets. Tell them I made a beautiful chart for them, but the planets are for Lucas and Evan.

"This is so great, Michelle," Cassie said. "Thank you for working so hard on this. We're going to win for sure!"

Mandy hugged Michelle.

Michelle couldn't tell them—she just couldn't. They were counting on her, and she couldn't let them down.

But she couldn't let Lucas and Evan down either.

What am I going to do? she wondered.

"Did you forget the aluminum foil?" Cassie asked.

"And our snacks?" Mandy added.

The foil, Michelle thought. The snacks.

The kitchen! Oh, no! Lucas and Evan are waiting for me to bring down the planets I painted.

Michelle slapped her forehead with her palm. "Yeah! I did. I can't believe it. I'll be right back."

I'm doomed! Michelle thought as she rushed out of her room and back down the stairs. What am I going to tell Lucas and Evan?

Michelle was so busy thinking about what she should do that she bashed right into Joey. She jumped in surprise.

Joey chuckled. "What planet are you on?" he joked.

"Very funny," Michelle muttered. Usually Joey's silly jokes made her feel better. But not today.

But maybe there was another way he could help her. "Joey, will you do me a favor?" Michelle asked.

"Let me hear it first," Joey said.

"All you have to do is go in the kitchen and say that watercolors are too pale. Say that neon paints would be better for planets. Okay?"

"Why?" Joey asked.

"I don't have time to explain. Just do it. Please?"

Joey shrugged. "Sure."

"Walk in a few seconds after me and go to the refrigerator or something. Okay?"

"Aye, aye, Captain." Joey gave her a salute.

Michelle hurried to the kitchen door. She scowled and made her eyes all squinty. I hope I look furious, she thought. She banged through the door.

"What's wrong?" Lucas exclaimed.

"The planets are gone," Michelle said.

"What?" Evan cried.

"I think Comet got them again," Michelle said. "There were pieces of crumbled Styrofoam all over the place."

51

Joey wandered into the kitchen and gave Evan, Lucas, and Michelle a big smile. Then he opened the refrigerator.

"I'll make some more planets," Michelle announced. "And I'll make sure Comet doesn't get them."

"Watercolors are too pale," Joey announced. He winked at Michelle.

Michelle glared back at him. He said it too soon!

"What?" Evan asked.

"Uh, I showed Joey the planets last night," Michelle lied.

"Really? You thought they looked too pale?" Lucas asked Joey. "What do you think we should use?"

"How about those really bright paints," Joey said. "What are they called, Michelle?"

"You mean neon paints?" Michelle asked.

"Yeah. Neon," Joey agreed.

"That's a great idea," Lucas said. "Michelle, do you have neon paints?"

Michelle nodded happily. "I'll go get them," she said. She turned toward the door.

Wait! She had to get snacks for Cassie and Mandy. She changed direction and headed for the refrigerator.

"The paints are in the fridge?" Evan asked.

Michelle froze. "Um . . . uh, no." She opened the fridge and pulled out a bowl of peaches. "These are for Comet," she said.

"Comet eats peaches?" Lucas asked. "I never heard of a dog who liked fruit."

"Uh, well, maybe he'll think these are the planets," Michelle said. "And then he won't eat any more of ours."

Lucas smiled. "Good idea," he said.

I'm getting pretty good at this lying, Michelle thought as she headed toward the stairs with the fruit. Now Cassie and Mandy will have pastel planets, and Evan and Lucas will have neon ones.

Michelle wished she had time to come up

with a better idea. But she didn't. She hoped the different colors would help.

"Hey," Cassie said. She started down the stairs toward Michelle. "I was just going to look for you. What took so long?" Cassie took the bowl of fruit from Michelle.

"Michelle? Don't forget the paint," Lucas called from the kitchen.

Michelle froze. Did Cassie hear Lucas?

Chapter

8

♥ "Who was that?" Cassie asked.

"Joey," Michelle answered. She began pushing her friend back up the stairs. She couldn't let Cassie find Lucas and Evan in the kitchen.

"That didn't sound like Joey," Cassie argued.

"He's working on some new voices for his show," Michelle lied.

"Why does he need paints?" Cassie asked.

"Um . . . he's painting something for the twins," Michelle said as she herded Cassie back into her room. "He wants my neon paints." Michelle rushed over to the closet and pulled out the paints.

"Those are great," Mandy said. "Can we use those for our display?"

"Joey needs them right now," Cassie explained. "He's painting something for Michelle's cousins."

Michelle bit her lip. She didn't like to hear her own lies coming from Cassie.

This is getting so out of control! I need to get rid of Lucas and Evan fast!

She pushed open the kitchen door and held out the paints. "Are they really neon?" Evan asked. He pulled open the jar of green paint.

"Yeah!" Michelle said. "And they will look great on the Styrofoam. Watch!" She picked up a plain ball and began to paint it green.

"Woof!" Comet came charging through

the kitchen. Oh, no. I forgot to close the door! Michelle realized.

Comet leapt up to grab the Styrofoam ball from Michelle's hand. His tail knocked over the jar of green paint on the counter.

It splashed everywhere. Green paint splattered all over the kitchen floor. It covered Comet's tail.

Michelle stared at the mess. She couldn't take it anymore. Every single thing she tried to do for this science contest went wrong. "That's it!" she yelled. "Comet—you're a bad dog. Go away! You're always messing everything up. *Get out!*"

Comet ran out of the room with his neon-green tail tucked between his legs. Michelle slammed the kitchen door behind him.

Lucas glanced at the clock. "It's almost dinnertime. I need to get home," he said. "Do you want us to help you clean up?"

"Uh, no," Michelle said. "You shouldn't

be late for dinner." She felt like pushing them both out the front door.

Lucas and Evan started to gather up their things. Michelle grabbed some paper towels and began to mop up the paint.

"What happened?" Mandy called. "We heard all that noise. Are you okay?"

She's heading for the kitchen, Michelle realized. "My sister," Michelle told the boys. "I don't want her to see this mess. She'll freak."

Michelle dashed out the kitchen door and shut it behind her. Then she leaned against it—just to be on the safe side. "Comet spilled Joey's paints, that's all."

"I'll help clean it up," Mandy offered, trying to push past Michelle.

"No!" Michelle yelped. "I mean—Joey's really angry, and Dad will be home any minute, and you should just go home, okay?"

"Okay, I guess." Mandy looked upset.

Michelle pushed her friend to the front door. "Can I get my stuff?" Mandy asked.

"Oh! Uh, sure," Michelle said.

As soon as Mandy disappeared at the top of the stairs, Michelle darted back into the kitchen and hustled the boys out the door. Then she ran up and hurried Mandy and Cassie off.

Michelle gave a deep sigh. She wished she could go out and ride her bike. She wanted to do something fun. Something that had nothing to do with the science contest.

But she couldn't. She had to clean the kitchen. She finished the job just as her father came in the back door. "Hi, Dad," Michelle said.

"Hi, sweetie. What happened?" he asked. He stared at the mound of paper towels covered in neon green paint.

"A paint disaster," Michelle said. "I'm sorry, Dad. Comet knocked over a jar of paint. It flew everywhere! It even splashed on his tail!"

"It's okay, honey," Danny answered, but his face turned pale. "But we need to go find him before he spreads paint all over the rest of the house."

Michelle followed her father out into the living room. She stopped short and stared at the front door.

"Why is the door open?" Danny asked.

Michelle didn't know what to say. She must not have closed it after she got both her teams out of the house.

"I hope Comet didn't get out," Danny said.

Suddenly Michelle remembered yelling at Comet. *Bad dog. Go away. Get out.*

Oh, Comet, no! Michelle thought. She ran into the front yard. "Comet!" she yelled. "Comet, I'm sorry. Come back!"

But Comet didn't come.

Chapter

9

♥ "Maybe Comet is still in the house," her father suggested.

"I'll go look." Michelle ran from room to room calling Comet's name.

This is all my fault, she thought. Poor Comet only wanted to play—and I was so mean to him.

Michelle ran back to the living room. "I can't find him anywhere, Dad!" Michelle told him. Her voice began to quiver.

"I can't either," her dad said.

"I left the door open, but I didn't mean for him to run away," Michelle said.

"I know that," Danny told her. "Don't worry, we'll find him."

"Find who?" Uncle Jesse asked as he and Aunt Becky came into the house with their arms full of groceries.

"Comet," Michelle told them. "He's missing!"

"Comet's missing?" Uncle Jesse cried. "What are we going to do?"

"We'll divide up and search for him. With all of us out there, I'm sure we'll find him," Aunt Becky said.

Aunt Becky always came up with good ideas. But Michelle had a horrible feeling that her plan wouldn't work. Comet ran away because *I* told him to, she thought. He doesn't *want* to come home.

"Michelle! You did more work on our project!" Mandy cried when Michelle arrived at school the next morning. She pointed to the pieces of poster board Michelle carried.

"Let's see!" Cassie said.

"That's not—" Michelle began.

"Hey!" Cassie cut her off. "This isn't our science project."

Cassie and Mandy stared at the poster. Michelle had drawn a picture of Comet. Underneath the picture she had written:

COMET COME HOME!

WE LOVE YOU!

GOLDEN RETRIEVER MISSING.

PLEASE CALL 555-2222.

BIG REWARD.

"Oh, no!" Mandy cried. "Is Comet lost? Michelle, this is terrible!"

"I'm so sorry Comet is missing," Cassie said.

"Comet loves you, Michelle," Mandy said. "He'll find his way home to you."

"You don't understand. I yelled at him for spilling that paint yesterday. That's why he ran away. My whole family spent hours searching for him—but we couldn't find him anywhere," Michelle said. Thinking about Comet made her feel like crying.

"He knows you didn't mean it," Cassie told her. "I yell at my cats sometimes, but they still want to sleep on my bed and everything."

Michelle tried to smile at her two best friends. She didn't want to talk about Comet anymore just then. "I'm sorry I'm not finished with all my stuff for our project," she said.

"We aren't either," Cassie told her. "Mandy and I are going to put together the model during our free hour." She pointed to a box at her feet. "We have everything with us."

The bell rang. "What free hour?" Michelle asked.

"Oh, yeah—I think you were in the bathroom," Mandy said. "Yesterday Mrs. Yoshida said we could have an hour to work on our projects today."

"Really?" Michelle squeaked. I didn't think I could feel any worse, she realized. But I do!

Michelle followed her friends into the classroom. As she took her seat, Lucas waved to her. He patted a big cardboard box by his seat—a big box with the words SCIENCE CONTEST STUFF written on the side.

Lucas expects me to work with him during the free hour too! Michelle put her head down on her desk. This is it. There is no way out. I'm about to lose all my friends!

Mrs. Yoshida took roll call. "Now we're going to have an hour of free study time," she announced. "Those of you who are entered in the Microsolid science contest can work on your projects. The rest of you may either read quietly or work on your spelling together."

"Michelle!" Cassie and Lucas called to her at the same time.

Michelle glanced at Cassie. Then she glanced at Lucas. There's only one thing to do, she thought.

She raised her hand.

"Mrs. Yoshida? I feel sick," Michelle called.

Chapter

10

♥ "Maybe you should take my temperature again," Michelle told the school nurse. She gave a little cough.

"I don't think you've developed a fever in the last two minutes," the nurse teased. "There is nothing wrong with you, Michelle."

I'm doomed, she thought. If the nurse doesn't send me home, Cassie and Mandy and Lucas and Evan will find out I'm on both teams.

"Why don't you tell me what's really

going on. Is there something else bothering you? Do you have a test?" the nurse asked.

"No," Michelle said.

"Trouble with your teacher?"

Michelle shook her head.

"Fight with your friends?"

"Nope," Michelle said. "I just don't feel well. I think I should go home."

"I can't send you home unless you're sick," the nurse said. "I'm sorry, but you'll have to return to your class."

Michelle shuffled back to Mrs. Yoshida's class as slowly as she could. There is no way out this time, she thought. I'll walk in the door and both teams will expect me to join them.

Where should I go first? Should I try to explain to Lucas and Evan? Or go straight to Cassie and Mandy and try to make them understand?

Cassie and Mandy, Michelle decided as

she entered the classroom. She made her way over to them and took a deep breath. "Hi!" she said. "I'm back."

Cassie glared at her. Mandy kept her eyes down.

Uh-oh! Michelle thought. They know! They already know I helped Lucas and Evan.

"Aren't you going to ask if I'm sick?" Michelle asked. She knew it was a dumb thing to say, but she couldn't think of anything else.

Cassie and Mandy stared at each other. Then they both stared at Michelle.

"We know what you did, Michelle!" Cassie snapped. "When Lucas saw our electric tie rack, he came over and said we stole the idea from you. We told him you were on our team. Then we found out you never quit *his* team!"

"You lied to us. You've been working with Lucas and Evan all along!" Mandy said angrily.

"And now there will be two solar system entries in the contest that are almost the same!" Cassie added.

"I'm sorry," Michelle cried. "I couldn't get out of working with them. And I didn't want you to be mad and . . ."

"Just forget it, Michelle," Mandy said. "We don't want to hear it."

"You're off the team," Cassie snapped.

"But we're best friends," she pleaded. "We do everything together. Remember?"

"Some best friend *you* are," Mandy said. "You wanted to win so badly that you worked on two teams. You wanted to double your chances of winning."

"What?" Michelle cried. "I don't care about winning! That isn't why I did this."

"Why don't you go work with Lucas," Mandy said. She turned her back on Michelle and continued working on her story about life on Neptune. Cassie turned her back too.

Michelle stood there for a minute. Her knees trembled, and she really did feel sick. Then she turned and walked over to Lucas and Evan.

"Traitor!" Lucas snapped.

Michelle gasped. "I am not," she said.

"A traitor is someone who gives away their team's good ideas. I can see from here that's what you did," Lucas said. "They even have an electric tie rack!"

"Spy!" Evan muttered.

"That's not fair. I know I should have told you I was working with Cassie and Mandy too. But I helped you as much as I helped them. I painted all those planets, and made you that map . . ."

"You're off the team," Lucas told her.

Lucas and Evan kept on writing in their notebooks. Neither one of them would look at her.

"Is there a problem, Michelle?" Mrs.

Yoshida asked her. Michelle shook her head and walked slowly back to her desk.

Not unless being called a traitor is a problem, Michelle thought.

Or losing Comet.

Or losing my two best friends.

Chapter

11

♥ "I didn't mean to work on both teams," Michelle admitted to her dad on Saturday morning—the day of the science contest. "It just happened."

She felt better now that she'd told him the whole story. Even the part about yelling at Comet.

Danny sat down next to her at the kitchen table. "Come on, Michelle," he said. "That's not exactly true, is it?"

Michelle stared down at the table. "No," she mumbled. "I could have told them the truth."

She gazed over at her father. "But I did a good job for both of them. I worked really hard so both projects would be good. I wanted Cassie and Mandy and Lucas and Evan to be happy. That's not really wrong, is it?"

"Sometimes trying to make everyone happy isn't the right thing to do," Danny told her. "Maybe Cassie and Mandy would have been angry with you if you didn't quit Lucas's team. But they are much angrier now because you stayed on the team *and* didn't tell them. All your work didn't make up for lying to them."

Michelle felt terrible. If only there was a way she could go back and fix everything.

I can't just apologize, she decided. I have to make everything better.

And I know exactly how to do it!

"Hey, Dad!" Michelle yelled. "I need you to drive me to Microsolid—right away!"

*   *   *

When Danny pulled the car up to the doors of Microsolid, the parking lot was completely empty.

"Are you sure it's open this early?" he asked.

"The flyer for the science fair said that kids could come anytime after nine A.M. to do any last-minute stuff on their projects," Michelle replied. "There should be a judge inside already."

"Okay, honey," Danny said. "Good luck with both your teams. The whole family will be back in time to hear the winners announced."

Michelle climbed out of the car and headed over to the building. Bright signs pointed the way to the science contest. When she entered the huge room, she spotted a tall woman reading a paperback book.

"I need to finish up my display," Michelle called. Her voice echoed.

"Let me know if you need anything," the

woman called back. "You're the first one here."

"Perfect!" Michelle whispered to herself. She needed some time without many people around.

She spotted a table with Lucas and Evan's display set up on top. Now I need to find Mandy and Cassie's stuff, she thought.

Michelle casually wandered up and down the rows of tables. I hope that judge won't wonder what I'm doing. Michelle turned the corner and found the pastel planets she had made for Cassie and Mandy.

Michelle grabbed a big box from under the table and packed everything from Cassie and Mandy's display inside. She shot a glance at the judge, but she was reading her book. She wasn't paying any attention to Michelle.

I'd better hurry. Michelle glanced at her watch. Cassie or one of the others could be here any second. She dragged the box over to the boys' table and unloaded it.

Now what? Michelle stared at all the pieces of the two projects. I know! I'll make a solar system with half pastel planets and half neon planets. That will look great!

She decided to use the pastel balls for the cold planets and the neon balls for the hot planets. She found the temperatures listed on Evan's science fact cards.

For the next hour, Michelle worked hard rearranging the solar system. When she finished, the pastel planets and neon planets spun together. A beautiful chart and map stood in back of the solar system. Mandy's stories about life on the planets and Evan's science facts were arranged on the tabletop.

It looks great! Michelle thought. She glanced around at the other projects in the big room. Most were completely set up now. And a lot more kids had arrived.

Mandy and Cassie and Lucas and Evan

should be here any minute. Michelle took a deep breath. I can't wait for them to see this. I know they're going to love it!

"Oh, no! I can't believe it!" someone yelled from behind her. "Michelle, what did you do?"

Chapter

12

♥ Michelle spun around. Lucas stood there, glaring at her.

Michelle backed away from the solar system. "I—" she began.

"You stole our solar system and gave it to your friends?" Lucas hollered before she could say another word.

"No! Let me explain—" Michelle began again.

"I can't believe you, Michelle. It's not bad enough you gave them our planets. Now you're giving them all our other stuff?"

"No," Michelle said. "Look!"

She pointed at the new nameplate she had made. The one that had Lucas's and Evan's names on it right next to Cassie's and Mandy's.

"It's better now," Michelle said softly. "It's one *great* solar system instead of two good ones. You all made it together. Now you're sure to win!"

Lucas didn't say anything. He just stared at the giant project.

"Doesn't it look great?" Michelle asked.

"Yeah, I guess so," Lucas said.

"What is this?" someone screamed. Michelle turned around and found herself staring straight into Cassie's angry face.

Cassie started yelling at Michelle.

Then Mandy showed up and started yelling.

Evan appeared and asked what all the yelling was about. When he saw the solar system, he started yelling too.

Michelle could see that they would all

keep yelling until the science contest started. She would never get them to listen to her. They would never let her explain about the one great solar system they had all built together.

Michelle quietly slipped away. She watched her friends yelling at one another from a corner of the room.

She watched as they all calmed down and peered at the new solar system.

Then she saw Mandy smile and point to the science facts and stories side by side. Evan smiled too.

Oh, well, Michelle thought. At least they like *something* I did.

A hush fell over the gym as the judges started studying all the projects. Michelle stayed in her corner. She held her breath as the judges approached the solar system.

She tried to figure out what they were thinking, but they kept their faces blank as they took notes. I wonder what they are writing in their little notebooks, she thought.

"Psst! Michelle!" Stephanie whispered. "Over here!"

Michelle turned to see her whole family standing along the wall near her. She rushed over to them.

"The solar system is beautiful!" D.J. said, giving Michelle a hug.

The judges took their places on the stage at one end of the room. Michelle crossed her fingers. She crossed her feet and tried to cross her toes.

The woman judge who had been on duty when Michelle arrived stepped up to the microphone. "Before I announce the winners, we wanted to tell you how impressed we were by all the entries here today. We think there are lots of future scientists out there—and we encourage you all to keep learning."

Michelle glanced over at Mandy, Cassie, Lucas, and Evan. They all looked nervous.

"Third place goes to 'Life on an Ant Farm,' " the judge announced. Twin girls ran up to the stage to get their certificate.

"Second place goes to 'Recycling Rewards,' " the judge said into the microphone. Four serious-looking boys hurried to the stage. They shook hands with the judge as she gave them their certificates.

"Now the project that will represent San Francisco in the state competition." The judge smiled. "First place goes to 'Our Solar System'!"

"Yes!" Lucas cried.

Mandy gave Cassie a hug.

Everyone started clapping and cheering.

I did it! Michelle thought happily. I really did it!

She had no friends. No dog. And no science project. But she helped build an award-winning solar system.

And both her ex-teams got what they wanted.

Cassie, Mandy, Lucas, and Evan rushed

up onto the stage. But they didn't take their certificates. Instead, everyone watched as they huddled together and whispered. When they came out of the huddle, Cassie approached the judge. They spoke for a moment, then the judge returned to the microphone.

"It seems there is one more member of this team. Michelle Tanner, would you please come up?"

Michelle gasped. She couldn't believe it. They weren't mad at her anymore! They wanted her on their team. She ran to them so fast that she almost tripped over her own feet.

"Thank you," she said to all her friends as the crowd clapped for them. "I'm really sorry."

Lucas led the way back to their display. Everyone congratulated them and told them what a great job they had done.

"I'm really sorry," Michelle said as soon

as they reached their table. "I should have told you the truth right away. But I thought I had figured out a way to work on both teams."

"I'm sorry too," Cassie said.

"Me too," Mandy agreed. "You really are a good friend."

"And you're right. Together we made a great solar system," Lucas said.

"Ice cream, anyone?" Danny came up to them. Michelle's whole family stood behind the solar system, smiling.

"It's up to the team," Michelle answered.

"Yes!" they all yelled.

"Maybe for Sacramento we can make a backdrop for our solar system mobile. We could have glow-in-the-dark stars," Lucas said.

"That sounds like a lot of work," Mandy said.

"Yeah. But now there are five of us to do it," Michelle said happily. "And I won't have to spend any time keeping the four of you apart!"

"But that's it, Michelle," Cassie told her. "Just the five of us. No one else. Even you can't be on *three* teams."

"Whoa! What's that?" D.J. cried when they turned the corner onto their street.

Michelle peered out the window. She caught a glimpse of something neon green glowing in the driveway. She rolled down the window and stuck her head out.

"It's Comet!" Michelle yelled.

"There's a car parked in our driveway," Danny cried. "Someone must have brought him home!" Everyone climbed out of the car.

"Hi. I'm Mrs. Soames from over on Elm Street," she said. "I think I have something that belongs to you." She let Comet's collar go and he scampered over to Michelle.

"Oh, Comet," Michelle said. She hugged the dog, burying her face in his fur.

"I never would have seen him in the dark if it weren't for that tail," Mrs. Soames said. "And then I remembered seeing your posters up all over town. He must have been roaming around for a day or two before I found him."

"I am so sorry, Comet," Michelle told the dog. "I'll never tell you to go away again— even if you eat all my planets!"

Slurp! Comet licked her face.

"Comet," Michelle said. "I don't care what anyone says. We are going to add one more member to our team. You are now the official mascot of the Cassie-Mandy-Lucas-Evan-Michelle solar system team!"

It doesn't matter if you live around the corner...
or around the world...
If you are a fan of Mary-Kate and Ashley Olsen,
you should be a member of

MARY-KATE + ASHLEY'S FUN CLUB™

Here's what you get:
Our Funzine™
An autographed color photo
Two black & white individual photos
A full size color poster
An official **Fun Club**™ membership card
A **Fun Club**™ school folder
Two special **Fun Club**™ surprises
A holiday card
Fun Club™ collectibles catalog
Plus a **Fun Club**™ box to keep everything in

To join Mary-Kate + Ashley's Fun Club™, fill out the form
below and send it along with

U.S. Residents – $17.00
Canadian Residents – $22 U.S. Funds
International Residents – $27 U.S. Funds

MARY-KATE + ASHLEY'S FUN CLUB™
859 HOLLYWOOD WAY, SUITE 275
BURBANK, CA 91505

NAME:_____

ADDRESS:_____

_CITY:_____ STATE:_____ ZIP:_____

PHONE:(____) _____ BIRTHDATE:_____

1242

FULL HOUSE™
Michelle

#1: THE GREAT PET PROJECT 51905-0/$3.50

#2: THE SUPER-DUPER SLEEPOVER PARTY
51906-9/$3.50

#3: MY TWO BEST FRIENDS 52271-X/$3.50

#4: LUCKY, LUCKY DAY 52272-8/$3.50

#5: THE GHOST IN MY CLOSET 53573-0/$3.99

#6: BALLET SURPRISE 53574-9/$3.99

#7: MAJOR LEAGUE TROUBLE 53575-7/$3.50

#8: MY FOURTH-GRADE MESS 53576-5/$3.99

#9: BUNK 3, TEDDY, AND ME 56834-5/$3.50

#10: MY BEST FRIEND IS A MOVIE STAR!
(Super Edition) 56835-3/$3.50

#11: THE BIG TURKEY ESCAPE 56836-1/$3.50

#12: THE SUBSTITUTE TEACHER 00364-X/$3.50

#13: CALLING ALL PLANETS 00365-8/$3.50

A MINSTREL® BOOK

Published by Pocket Books

FULL HOUSE™
Stephanie

PHONE CALL FROM A FLAMINGO	88004-7/$3.99
THE BOY-OH-BOY NEXT DOOR	88121-3/$3.99
TWIN TROUBLES	88290-2/$3.99
HIP HOP TILL YOU DROP	88291-0/$3.99
HERE COMES THE BRAND NEW ME	89858-2/$3.99
THE SECRET'S OUT	89859-0/$3.99
DADDY'S NOT-SO-LITTLE GIRL	89860-4/$3.99
P.S. FRIENDS FOREVER	89861-2/$3.99
GETTING EVEN WITH THE FLAMINGOES	52273-6/$3.99
THE DUDE OF MY DREAMS	52274-4/$3.99
BACK-TO-SCHOOL COOL	52275-2/$3.99
PICTURE ME FAMOUS	52276-0/$3.99
TWO-FOR-ONE CHRISTMAS FUN	53546-3/$3.99
THE BIG FIX-UP MIX-UP	53547-1/$3.99
TEN WAYS TO WRECK A DATE	53548-X/$3.99
WISH UPON A VCR	53549-8/$3.99
DOUBLES OR NOTHING	56841-8/$3.99
SUGAR AND SPICE ADVICE	56842-6/$3.99
NEVER TRUST A FLAMINGO	56843-4/$3.99
THE TRUTH ABOUT BOYS	00361-5/$3.99